Joy Resor

Designed to SHINE!
Read Aloud Rhymes for Any Size Heart

by Joy Resor
Joy On Your Shoulders
P.O. Box 951
Pisgah Forest, NC 28768

Find Joy on the Web: joyonyourshoulders.com

Copyright © 2018 by Joy On Your Shoulders

Illustrator: Lauren Connell
Book Design: Blue Sun Studio, Inc.
bluesunstudio-inc.com

ISBN: 978-0-9840353-4-2

Designed to SHINE!

Read Aloud Rhymes for Any Size Heart

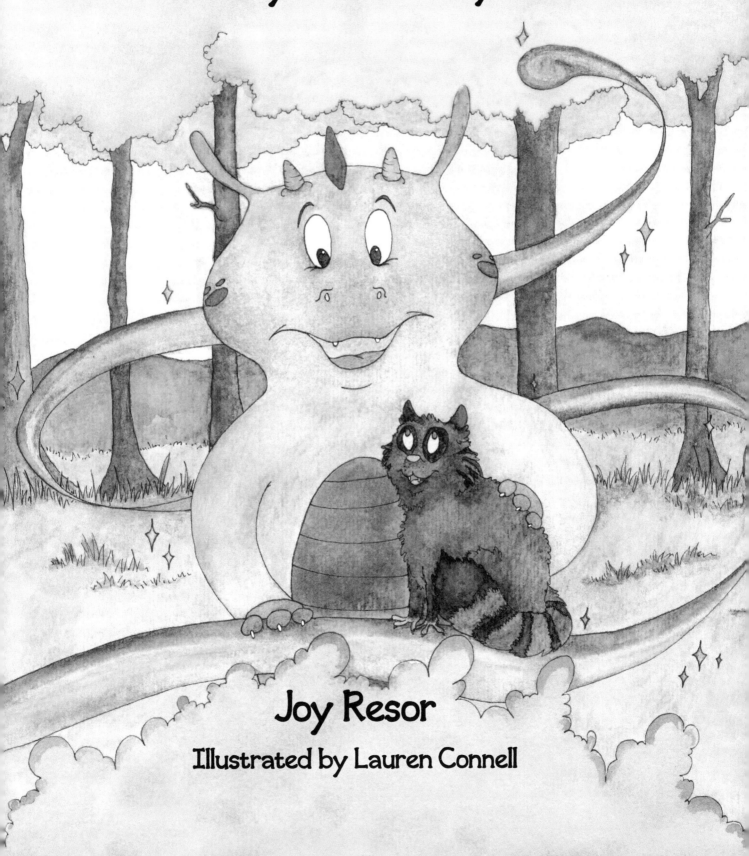

Joy Resor

Illustrated by Lauren Connell

Introduction

May *Designed to SHINE! Read Aloud Rhymes for Any Size Heart* allow you and your children or your inner child to gather closer and to laugh longer as you talk about the topics.

Take turns reading! Play! Enjoy!

I imagine you'll read one topic a day, three or nine...however this book works in a full house or for you living alone.

May the ideas, values and gratitude expressed support your own.

May you feel lighter, more in love with life and more peaceful.

Allow the book to lead you where it does...to extending extra kindness within or without, to writing a poem, to dancing with your son...

Designed to SHINE! arrived through my heart and hands with ease and delight.

May the spirit in which this book entered be present as you enjoy its humor, rhythm and wisdom on your own or with a child on your lap or by your side.

Dear one, I am grateful to create this book for you, because it responds to a call within my soul for us to enjoy life, and because it was so much fun to write.

To our love, peace and joy.

Love,

Joy

Attention

Attention, Attention
Pay ATTENTION - YOU!

Today sparkles NEW
WITH A BRIGHT, SHINY VIEW.

It's FRESHER than FRESH
CLEANER than CLEAN!

Close your eyes, take a breath.
Do you see what I mean?

Are you ready to go?
Are you set for a treat?

THIS DAY OF ALL DAYS
Will NEVER repeat!

Make it GRAND, Make it fine
It's yours to design.

In your Heart, in your mind

ENJOY ITS BRIGHT SHINE!

Balance

BALANCE a book
On your head if you dare.

Then slip your left toe
Under Scully's pet bear!

BALANCE your days
Running outside and in.

Busy, so active
Then time to tuck in.

Not all of one thing
Like climbing all day

Or skimming away
In a skiff near a ray.

But days lived in BALANCE
With good time to spare

To breathe extra long
IN YOUR BALANCING CHAIR!

3

4

Change

CHANGE, we all feel it
It's how the world rocks.

Tight tulips that open
Clock hands which tick tock!

A seal on the corner
Who likes your green hat.

The one who is waving
Before sliding...KERSPLAT!

CHANGE is forever
It's how the world turns.

You fliggle or wiggle
In flow as you learn!

Sulking and screaming
Don't CHANGE CHANGE a bit

But breathing through CHANGE
LETS SMILES GENTLY FIT!

Dance

To music outside you
To songs that you sing.

With others or solo
To DANCE is the thing!

It's more fun than ever
To let yourself move.

Stretch upward, kick outward
Get into a groove.

Now bend at the waist
In ways that feel great.

Yes, DANCE on this day
With shimmy and shake!

Your body will glimmer
Like stars at night shine.

Then snag a sweet spot
TO RECLINE YOUR BEHIND!

Energy

Candles and light bulbs
Fuel to run cars.

Peddling with Pandas
Flying to Mars.

Name all the ENERGY
You see and you know.

Have you felt a bit weak
When your ENERGY's low?

Is it time to hold onto
The kitten you love?

Or splash through a puddle
Of rain from above?

Are you goofily giggling
While tickling a shrew?

What is your ENERGY
ASKING OF YOU?

Forgive

Did you make a mistake?
It's easy to do.

Did you trip your hyena
Or paint his face blue?

Did you spray sis with a hose
Or skip with a skunk?

End up in trouble
Feel all in a funk?

No problem, no issue
No worry, no harm.

The best thing to do
Is to sound NO alarm!

But calm yourself down
Love who you are.

Say that you're sorry
OUT LOUD TO THE STARS!

Grateful

Oh, to be GRATEFUL
Thanking life for all things.

All people, all nature.
A tree's many rings.

Cloud shapes in the sky.
The sun on your face.

Roses and robins.
Spring gifts of pure grace.

The hen on her eggs.
A dog by your feet.

All that we are
As well as sweet treats.

GRATEFUL so matters.
I'll show you the way

To fill up your heart
WITH THE GIFTS OF TODAY!

Happy

Do you hang out with folks
Who knock this and that?

Where negative words
Can feel like a path?

Not here, Mister Mole
Not here, Sister Slug.

You don't have to settle
For feelings that bug!

There's no need to tiptoe
Past Peter Pout Pout.

Or wrestle your HAPPY
From sisters who shout.

To the island of HAPPY.
I'm sailing there now.

Give yourself HAPPY.
YOUR SEATS BY THE COW!

15

Imagine

IMAGINE your way
Wherever you can.

To a cave, to a farm
To your own Fairyland.

Grab bubbles, add blocks
Drink cocoa, eat toast.

Let mermaids lead Monday
To long ago coasts.

Have fun, sink inside
This magical spin.

To your heart, to your toes
Do you feel yourself grin?

Create as you do
Spread bread crumbs or not.

IMAGINE your way
GIVE IT ALL THAT YOU'VE GOT!

Joy

A feeling so high
So bold and so deep.

It's natural, normal
Your birthright to keep.

Meet essence of JOY
On a walk in the creek.

Then stepping on grass
In tender barefeet.

Greet JOY by yourself
Or with badgers nearby.

With monkeys on treetops
Geese streaming through sky.

Add hula in sunbeams
Do not hesitate.

Share it, embrace it
TO JOY CELEBRATE!

Kindness

When KINDNESS appears
Does she feel like a pup?

Who nuzzles your chin
When you hold her close up?

Does your skin kind of tingle
Your heart skip a beat?

Do you squeal with such glee
When she nuzzles your feet?

Yes, KINDNESS, oh KINDNESS
We love your sweet shine.

To feel you, to hold you
We know you're DIVINE!

KINDNESS shines golden.
KINDNESS runs free.

TO KINDNESS IN YOU!
TO KINDNESS IN ME!

Love

From kisses at bedtime
To squeezing your Gram.

LOVE touches your insides
Sends hearts to SHAZAM!

LOVE offers you gifts
Like a fluffy white chick.

Or cuddles you tighter
At night when you're sick.

LOVE shows up as action
In words and in smiling.

It rises at dawn
Without even trying.

LOVE LOVES you, no doubt
How tall you will grow.

LOVE'S happy you're YOU
WITH YOUR MAGICAL GLOW!

24

Magic

Is there MAGIC today
In a card trick you played?

Or a prism in sun
Splashing colors this way?

MAGIC is here when
You see it or wish

For a carnival ride
On a boat that's a fish.

MAGICAL music
That makes your knees bend.

Stories that call
To far lands of pretend.

MAGICAL monkeys with
Tails that tell tales.

Dolphins that dally
ON MARSHMALLOW WHALES!

Nature

Forests of pine trees
Redbuds of pink.

Lightning bug nights
You watch their lights blink.

Squirrels on a tree
Ducks quacking away.

A field full of horses
Who eat lots of hay.

Sheep sheared for wool
Sweet grass in our toes.

Parks to ride bikes
Rivers to row.

The sweet earth below us
The blue sky above.

A world overflowing
WITH NATURE TO LOVE!

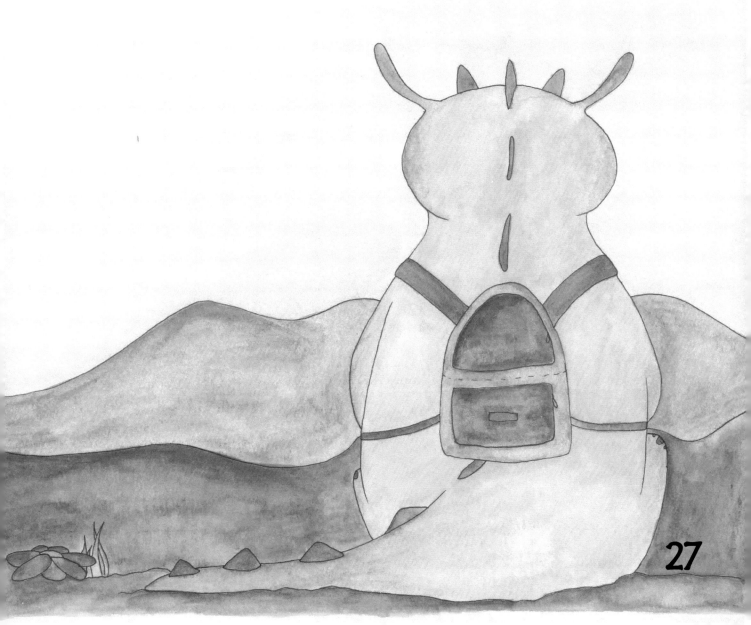

OPEN

OPEN your feelings
So love can come in.

The door to a castle
Where kingdoms begin.

OPEN a window
To welcome a breeze.

OPEN a tissue
To catch the next sneeze.

OPEN a book
Whenever you can.

Adventure is calling
Discover new lands.

OPEN hearts wide
When a rainbow is near.

Skip to the window
WITH JOY AS YOU CHEER!

PEACE

PEACE in your heart
Your soul and your mind.

PEACE in your family
While waiting to dine.

Breathe into PEACE
As you sit near a tree.

Speak 'round a fire
Your voice – oh so free.

PEACE to all beings
Because we all matter.

Blue birds and black bats
Reindeer who clatter.

Sink into PEACE
As a seed that you sow.

With PEACE in your heart
KINDNESS ALWAYS WILL FLOW!

QUIET

Whisper in places
Where loud doesn't fit.

Tiptoe to bedtime
When open eyes quit.

Talk in soft tones when
Weak voices are sore.

Relax as you know
That rest is the cure.

Quietly walk
Up lanes you love so.

To visit Old Doc
And the roses he grows.

Read in a corner
With family aware

Or quietly sit
Next to Aunt Clara's chair.

RASCALS

Big Bad Wolf charts
A good place to start.

Who huffed and who puffed
Blowing houses apart.

RASCALS are shifty
They're meant to add risk.

The point is not naming
The idea now is this --

Harness your own
RASCALLY actions, my dear.

No tripping your brother
Or adding to fear.

Leave RASCALS in movies
In Zombies, in plays.

Make choices that add
MORE LIGHT TO YOUR DAYS!

SHINE

Today marks the start
To SHINE as a light

Which starts deep inside
Where peace makes it bright.

What steps can you take
To polish this SHINE?

Write poems, take walks
Watch ants march in line?

Your soul knows the path
Your soul speaks within.

It calls in the night
It loves to begin.

To SHINE through your smile
To speak in your heart.

Allow your bright SHINE
TODAY IS THE START!

Time

Are days a big rush?
Is there too much to do?

Can you take a fresh look
At TIME'S Rusharoo?

Consider a change
Get set in the night.

Turn oh dear, not morning
Into one of delight.

Add ease, add a game
Allow time to play.

TIME loves to expand
With joy through the day.

Be present, wake up
To moments, my dear.

Then TIME is a blessing
A REASON TO CHEER!

Untie

UNTIE sad feelings.
Scrumbumbly ones too.

They don't need to stay
In the being of you.

Release them through tears,
Through pencils, through art.

UNTYING the iglies
Means much to your heart.

Perhaps with a friend
Or a teacher you know.

Follow the feelings
That call to your soul.

UNTIE them, UNTIE them.
You'll feel better soon.

Your insides will shine
LIKE SUN-SPLASHED FULL MOON!

Vacation

VACATION, Playcation.
A feeling so great.

VACATION means
Days in a row to create.

It gives you more time
More space and more ease

To run through a meadow
To honor the trees.

You could travel inside
Your mind with a book.

Or travel to Grandpa's
Catch fish on a hook.

VACATION unfolds
With designs you can test.

Relax your whole self
AS YOU SINK INTO REST!

Wonder

WONDER oh WONDER.
We treasure you so!

Surprise and deep awe
The amazement we know.

You invite us to notice
Through buds and in snails.

In clouds that float past
In elephant tails.

You flash us with lightning
You holler in stars.

You open our hearts
To reach for high bars.

WONDER, oh WONDER.
We thank you...hooray!

You skip old routines
TO BRIGHTEN OUR DAYS!

45

X-ray

When we X-RAY our days
What bones do they show?

Are they zipping by fast
Are they crawling with slow?

Can you simply agree
To ways this day goes?

Might you say you'll begin
To stop naming your woes?

Is it time to release
A stuck way you act

Or offer forgiveness
When lunch isn't packed?

Let's X-RAY this day
Adding grace to its bones

Then watch it expand
INTO FULL LOVING TONES!

Yes

You may hear more no
Than YES as you flow.

It's how some adults
Take a lead as you grow.

They decide against things
Setting limits for you.

And YES with its ease
Could be skipped; it's true.

Try YES in an answer.
Say YES to your Mom.

And watch how her YES
Flips quickly to on!

With swiftness you sit
When she asks you to rest.

Bringing smiles for miles
IN THIS YES MOMMY FEST!

49

Zest

ZEST could mean spice
That's added to meat.

Or an Antelazoon
Who steps on your feet.

ZEST comes to your heart
Like an inner idea

As gratitude grows
For ways that are dear.

When life zips along
With fun on the side

And friends who stop in
Bring airplanes that glide.

It's a Spirit that's light.
It's a path lit this way.

Add spice as you can
ICING ZEST TO YOUR DAYS!

Afterword

For decades, I felt a deep sense of not belonging to myself, my family or the world, hiding in clothes too large, not speaking up in gatherings and feeling less than others.

In my 30's, I daily wrote a prayer to become the Joy I am created to be.

Divinity led me to books, classes and healers, guiding me into ever-evolving versions of the Joy I am.

These days, I am a loving, peaceful, joy-filled being who receives books to inspire readers and whose presence brings light.

This book that came through me as a wise and fun treasure feels destined to reach more people than anything I've so far created. Since it's self-published, your support is more valuable than you may know.

If you love this book, please spread word, write reviews and share it with friends in person and on social media to send *Designed to SHINE! Read Aloud Rhymes for Any Size Heart* deeply into the world to bless children, families and all who receive its gifts.

And...be on the lookout within the next year for *Designed to SHINE! Read Aloud Rhymes for Any Size Heart—Book 2*

The second volume swiftly arrived after the first with 26 new rhyming topics like AMAZE, BELIEVE, CREATE, DREAM, EXTRA, FROSTING...

Thank you, dear reader.

To all the ways we LOVE and SHINE!

Joy

About the Author

Joy Resor shines in western North Carolina where she writes books that inspire readers, serves clients in spiritual direction, leads classes and loves life moment by moment. Daily grateful that she lives beyond wounds that kept her hiding, Joy leans into new adventures that call to her soul.

joyonyourshoulders.com

About the Illustrator

Lauren Connell is an artist who loves to illustrate the whimsical world around her. She works in a multitude of mediums, from watercolor to print-making. She lives in North Georgia with her farm animals and family, hiking and traveling whenever she can. The outdoors are a great influence on her work and keep her inspired.